The Suicide
of Robert

SHEILA ROBINSON

The Suicide of Robert, Second Edition

ISBN: 978-1-938373-15-2

Table of Contents

Scripture References

Chapter 2: 2 Samuel 16:20-17:1-23
Chapter 3: 1 Samuel 31:1-6; 2 Samuel 1:1-10
Chapter 4: 1 Kings 16:8-19

Foreword

The task of the theologian is to interrogate the language of the church to see where it both portrays and betrays the Gospel message. Some of the most gifted theologians that history has recorded undertake this task with a hermeneutic of hunger that the Bible is read as the answer to what oppression, illness, lack of education, and apathy inflict on human beings (Soelle 2001). In this volume, Pastor Sheila Robinson, DMin, masterfully applies a hermeneutic of hunger to the Sacred Text in a most imaginative way. Woven through it is the biblical testimony in dialogue with contemporary issues, the intersection of which helps the reader critique their suppositions and beliefs about some timeless themes.

The subject of suicide has been a source of pain for all parties involved as long as humanity has faced our mortality. The existential questions of life and the afterlife have been complicated by theological dialogue that has failed to show the sensitivity and nuance that such a delicate matter demands. In this book, we are led into a conversation regarding theodicy, hope, soteriology, eschatology, human fragility, pain, and redemption and invited to think through the complex and fundamentally human questions that suicide engenders in a sensitive, yet engaging way.

The human condition is universal, and it is essential to the faith of the followers of Jesus that human behavior has eternal consequences. This amazing scholar and theologian has found a way to deal with the complexities of universal human behaviors with the most accessible language. Through the power of story, we are gifted with her insights into the heart of God and the condition of humankind, affirming the Gospel message of grace and hope, while never disavowing choice and consequence. The sacred tension between free will and the foreknowledge of God, questions about death and dying, hope and hopelessness are all given serious attention while the reader is engulfed in a fictional narrative. In the tradition of *Pilgrim's Progress* and *The Screwtape Letters,* this literary offering is a theological treatise wrapped in narrative.

As a constructive theologian with a liberative lens, I may not enter the conversation from the same place, but I am excited about this work and its contribution to human flourishing. As the reader is invited into this conversation, I pray that the Spirit will speak through the writing into the heart and imagination of each individual. Let these finely written words guide you into the questions that unlock the very heart of God.

Bishop Edward Donalson III, DMin
Director of Liturgy and Worship
Seattle University

Dedication

The act of suicide, the deliberate ending of one's life, is deeply rooted in the human passions of disappointment, desperation, hopelessness, and other despairing and overwhelming emotions. Entwining itself into the thoughts and psyche of human beings for millennia, suicide has all too frequently presented itself as a reasonably appropriate option, a final and concrete alternative for a circumstance or set of circumstances that seem too complex and severe to be resolved. When pressing issues appear irreparable or permanently unsolvable, suicide is a response to the perception that no corrective options are available, and no viable alternatives are present. Thus, the act looms large in the fractured mind of its victim as the only step left to take.

Suicide is not only a devastatingly futile act for that victim, but for those who are left behind to mourn, grieve, wrestle with guilt, and otherwise attempt to make sense of the victim's self-murder; this deliberate and final act leaves an unbearably emotional juxtaposition of anger, pain, and heartache.

In some cases, however, based on cultural traditions and place in history, suicide is considered an honorable, valiant course of action. Or, sometimes, it is seen as a deed that allows the victim to save face and avoid the dishonor of being openly disgraced. By simply choosing to end their life, a person may seek to bring a definitive close to a situation considered dishonorable.

Therefore, this book is dedicated to all those who have considered or attempted suicide and failed. It is also dedicated to the memory of those who have succeeded: To the teens and young adults who were the victims of bullying or other serious aggressions and chose this way of escape when the hostility became too much; this book remembers you. To the persons who lived same-gender loving or other alternative lifestyles but committed suicide when the trauma, judgment, and complexities became more than they could bear, this book has you in mind. To the women who chose suicide instead of life under the harshness of the male-dominated practices of their c culture, this book remembers your pain. And, to the isolated, misguided 8-year-old who, out of child-like but genuine love for his mother, chose suicide to oblige her thoughtless verbalization of a wish that she had "one less mouth to feed," this book cries for you.

And finally, this book is dedicated to pastors who helped so many others, but could not help themselves when they reached their own breaking point of complete helplessness. Instead, they turned to suicide as their final solution when it seemed as though enough was simply enough! This book was written with you in mind with deep
respect, sorrow, and a desire to honor your struggles and your service."

Chapter 1
The Decision

Robert was a Pastor. And he found himself at a severely crucial crossroad in his life as both a minister and a man. He pastored The Church of Faith and Hope, a growing church in an area where people viewed church attendance as a natural and acceptable way of life. The departments and auxiliaries within the congregation were not only growing in membership but thriving in their calendar of events and activities. On the surface, it appeared that everything was operating smoothly and that all was well within the walls of The Church of Faith and Hope. But Robert knew better. Everything was, in fact, not well.

Truth be told, Robert's life was in a state of complete shambles, and try as he might, he had been unable to resolve any of his ever-increasing crises and hurtful disappointments. He was relentless in his efforts to bring in finances so that the much-needed modern improvements could be made to the church structure to increase its value and improve its visual appeal. The financial inflow had decreased dramatically since the scandal of Robert's alleged misappropriation of the church's funds had erupted.

Former generous donors were declining his requests for additional funds and, in some cases, refusing to even accept his calls. As a result of these impediments, Robert's financial calamities were escalating at an alarming rate, and his once impeccable reputation was fast becoming severely tarnished. In place of his once- polished image emerged contrived allegations, false accusations, tampered documents, and a series of looming indictments.

The Executive Board of the church had contacted his Presiding Bishop demanding Robert's resignation. His dearest and closest friends were suspicious of him and had begun casting aspersions on his integrity and honesty. His wife, Julia, and other family members had even begun to need constant reassurance from him that the assertions were untrue. But most hurtful, Bob Jr., Robert's only son with whom he shared a wonderfully warm and trusting father-son relationship, was now expressing doubt about his father's innocence in all these matters. "Surely, Dad, everyone can't be lying, what's up?" were the words still ringing in Robert's ears from early this morning when Bob Jr. first challenged his father. And for Robert, this was the last straw.

His son's doubt concerning his innocence was more than Robert could handle; there seemed to be nothing left at this point. "Could anything else possibly go wrong?" he questioned himself. Had God forsaken him? Wasn't God going to intervene and come to his rescue? He was feeling the most helpless and hopeless that he had ever felt in his entire life. He couldn't bear much more of the pain associated with his present state of being, which seemed entirely too complicated and too convoluted to unravel for the truth of his innocence to be revealed.

Robert found himself entertaining thoughts of suicide, but quickly dismissed those thoughts as spiritually and scripturally inappropriate. He was a Pastor and had preached against the notion of suicide, labeling it an absolutely unreasonable and groundless option in the face of adversity. He had taken a firm stand against suicide, saying it should never be named as a resolve worthy of consideration for life's dilemmas. He had sat with and counselled others who were contemplating suicide and had convinced them that suicide was not the answer. Yet here he was giving serious thought to suicide himself.

And as frequently as he dismissed his suicidal thoughts, they just as frequently returned. "Oh my rescuing God, where are You?" was Robert's recurring yet unanswered question. Where was the God who had readily entered the flames of Shadrach, Meshach, and Abednego's inferno, walked with them in the fire, and brought them out of the furnace unscathed with not so much as a smell of smoke or a trace of having ever been near a fire, much less in one? Robert's torment was unbearable as he cried aloud, "God, I'm in a financial fire, where are You?" Still, God was silent.

He tried reasoning with himself by allowing his mind to reflect on some of his own commentaries on the subject. "Suicide doesn't resolve anything…" "Maintain your integrity to stand your ground firmly and face your problems…" "Things are never quite bad enough to justify suicide…" "Suicide can support the notion that you are, in fact, guilty." Despite all of Robert's former advice to others, he found himself completely incapable of listening to and acting upon his own counsel. Because he saw no reprieve in sight, he felt trapped, alone, betrayed, desperate, and overwhelmed. He simply could not face another day. His decision was made; he would end his life.

He drove his car to the bridge, stopped midway, pulled the car over to the bridge railing, turned the ignition off, and absentmindedly left the door open as he got out. He walked around the rear of the car and stood at the apex of the bridge. Leaning on the pedestrian railing, he looked over the rail to view the waters below and stared down into the darkness of the night. In his effort to see through the black openness below the bridge, it appeared as though the atmosphere and everything around him were working in concert to purposely prevent him from seeing what lay just beneath his visual acuity.

He knew this segment of the river was its deepest and most turbulent point; hence the bridge. Yet a clear and distinct view of the water below eluded him as though it had faded into silent nothingness. The quiet stillness was deafening. The usual sound of the rhythmic surging and lapping of the water was noticeably absent, almost as if the river was no longer present or had made a deliberate decision to be completely noiseless. But Robert was not to be distracted by any of these conditions. He had come to the bridge for a specific purpose, and he was not going to be diverted from his primary intent.

He cautiously lifted his left leg onto the pedestrian railing of the bridge, careful to keep his balance. He didn't want to make a misstep and inadvertently fall backward onto the concrete ground just to end up living with a debilitating head impairment or a crippling back injury. Lifting his other leg, he exercised precision to make sure he had firm footing of both feet on the railing so that his final act would be one of exact and premeditated control. Once in a full standing position on the railing, Robert felt a strange sense of freedom. If only he could stand like this forever, feeling the freedom of being unencumbered and unrestricted by all things tangible. The still silence engulfed him, embraced him, and beckoned him into its soundless abyss. Robert yielded. He opened wide his arms, closed his eyes, and leaned forward into the blackness facing him. He felt himself falling headfirst into space, fully anticipating the weight of his airborne body to fling him thunderously into the icy waters awaiting him so that all of his troubles would be finally over.

Then abruptly, the impossible happened. He was no longer falling, but was hanging weightlessly in midair in an upright position, suspended there as if caught between floors in an elevator. But there was no elevator, there was no floor, no firm substance of any sort, there was no ground to support his feet underneath him, not even the water. He opened his eyes, looked around, and saw nothing. He began to frantically flail his feet in search of something to identify his dangling and confusing whereabouts.

He was desperate for something that would provide the stability of firmness upon which he could stand. Thrashing about, his feet in tandem with his legs began acting involuntarily on their own behalf, frantically reaching for the safety and support of firm grounding. But there was none. Instead, there was only the non-supportive uncertainty of empty space. In this strange situation, Robert found himself glaringly and obviously absent of any sort of safety net. How was this possible? As he floundered about in the air, terrified of what was happening, he heard a stern and authoritative voice, but saw no one. Yet the commanding voice told him, "Be still!"

Chapter 2
The First Encounter

Immediately, Robert obeyed the voice. Everything within him responded, even his legs and feet ceased to uncontrollably wave about. His entire being became instantly motionless as if frozen in space and time. He stood still, there in the air at a midway point between the bridge above and the river below.

The voice from nowhere began to speak to him again, this time, however, it spoke with a more entreating manner. "Hello Robert," it said, "my name is Ahithophel. You may remember me from your sacred text. The story of my situation is briefly mentioned in the segment of your sacred text that you have identified as the second book of Samuel. We, in antiquity, have always been fascinated by the fact that the writers of your early civilization divided the chronicles of Prophet Samuel into two separate books, to which you have given the categories of first and

second, almost as if there were two separate Prophets, each with the name Samuel. Nevertheless, to complete my assigned task with you with precision and accuracy, I will tell you my story as it is contained in the portion of the prophet's epic known to you as
Second Samuel, in chapters 16 and 17."

"I was among the men who rode with Absalom, King David's son, in our search for King David. It was Absalom's plan when he found his father to kill him and take over his throne and power. We had arrived in Jerusalem and were discussing strategies for the continued search and ultimate capture of King David when Absalom turned to me and asked my advice. I replied that by disparaging the name and character of King David, it would go a long way in helping Absalom gain favor in the hearts and minds of the people. I suggested the best way to do this was for him to openly go into his father's wives' tents for everyone to see."

"In your 21st-century language, Robert, you would say 'sleep with' his father's wives. And because my reputation for exercising sound and exact counsel was known and well respected among the people, even King David himself, Absalom, followed my instructions to the letter and did exactly as I advised.

He went into his father's wives, or slept with them as you would say, and he did so one by one in full open view for all to see. What an awful and most disrespectful reproach that was to King David."

"I was quite pleased with myself and felt a sense of pride that my suggestion had been so well received and carried out with such predictable responses from the people. They were horrified that Absalom, the son of King David, had done such a thing, especially since the actions of David's son were a direct reproach on David himself. I was feeling quite full of myself and took advantage of the fact that my advisory counseling was so exact and true to my words, so much so that I was considered to have been an oracle of God."

"My warnings and admonishments whenever I spoke were thought to have come directly from our God. And because I had just been so successful in accomplishing my goal of tarnishing King David's good name through the despicable acts of his son Absalom, I couldn't remain satisfied with that victory alone. I felt the need to press Absalom even further with what I considered to be even greater advice. I persuaded him to permit me to choose twelve thousand men to attack King David that very night. I supposed he would have reached his point of discouragement and sheer exhaustion by this time from having had to elude the severe and concentrated chase of his beloved son Absalom. I reasoned that David would panic at my attack, and his faithful soldiers who were with him would turn and run away. The plan was to use that opportunity to kill David since he was the target of Absalom's search."

"The plan was brilliant, so I thought, but this time Absalom sought additional counsel from Hushai to see if he agreed with my plan or had a different strategy. As it turned out, Hushai disagreed with my scheme, saying it was not a good one. He reminded Absalom of the great and cunning abilities that King David possessed in war tactics, the unbeatable bravery of David's soldiers combined with their intense loyalty to him, and finally, David's stunning history of defeating his enemies. Hushai offered Absalom an entirely different conspiracy than I had offered. I was shocked and dismayed that Absalom took Hushai's plan to heart over mine, but more than anything else, I was desperately afraid. It was immediately at that point that I realized and knew without the slightest doubt that my life was in peril. Therefore, with no other choice, so I thought, I returned home, arranged my affairs in order, and came to the same conclusion you just reached, Robert. I took my life. I hanged myself."

Bewildered, Robert could not fathom what was happening. As the haunting voice of Ahithophel continued, he heard Ahithophel say that he had been sent to this place in time to tell him how wrong his decision was. "It is not the will of God," Ahithophel said, "that you should end your life." Ahithophel continued, "I didn't learn what I am about to tell you until it was too late, and it very well might be too late for you also, Robert. But I am going to tell you anyway because God sent me here to do so. God loves us all so very much and does not wish for us to feel the kind of hopelessness that drives us to end our lives. He desires to walk with us through our bleak moments so that we can eventually see His hand in our deliverance and hear His instructions for our way out of what may seem like an inescapably destructive situation."

"The thought in our mind that tells us to go ahead and kill ourselves before our enemy takes the opportunity to do so is an evil scheme. It comes directly from the wicked and malevolent heart of Satan. When we fail to reject Satan's whisperings by giving in to his urgings to take our own lives, we completely discount the power and sovereignty of God to intervene for us on our behalf. When we believe that Satan's vile and lying tongue speaks truth, that his murderous temptations of self-destruction are our only options, that our problems have enlarged to overwhelming and insurmountable proportions, we remove all possibilities that our problems might be resolvable. And what is most devastating, we deny the Power of God to manifest itself and come through as the all-powerful delivering source that it is. This happens because we neither seek nor rely on our loving God for direction. And this is what you have done, Robert. I know this because I felt the same way. I felt hopeless and powerless."

"But after hanging myself, I became so very full of sorrow. I had taken the safety and future of my life into my own hands and acted upon the senselessness of my cowardly thoughts instead of allowing God to work out His plan for me. And instead of remaining alive to face the consequences of my behavior like a man of strength that I thought I was, I took the cowardly way out. I therefore find myself continuing to apologize to God many times over for my **self-murder**. These facts that I'm sharing with you, are the reasons you are suspended here in this place at this time. I hope you are learning something from my visit with you. I don't know God's plan for you or what the outcome will be of your actions tonight. I simply know I was summoned by God to come and speak to you based on my experiences. So farewell, Robert. I hope I won't be seeing you soon; instead, I hope God has something miraculous in store for you."

Chapter 3
The Second Encounter

Robert was struggling to come to grips with what was going on around him. Ahithophel had left as abruptly as he had appeared, all the while being invisible yet fully present and audible. He had accused Robert of being a coward, unwilling to stand up like a man and face his circumstances and receive the consequences of his behavior.

Quickly and defensively, Robert began to defend himself.

"I did try to stand up for myself, from the very beginning, I tried to answer my accusers and refute their accusations. But matters only continued to become worse as the mounting evidence became a more incriminating assemblage of proof testifying against me. Try as I may, I could not establish my innocence. I just seemed to sink deeper into the quagmire of accusations that screamed my guilt. But was Ahithophel correct? Am I a coward? Did I desert myself and my case at the height of my battle? Did I abandon the task given to me to stand against the injustices of wrongful guilt, no matter what?"

Robert fired these questions at himself in search of the real truth about the matter, all the while hoping and expecting to hear someone fire back the answers of his innocence. But there was no one there. Ahithophel had gone, and Robert hung there in space in the blackness of the night, alone. It seemed now to him that Ahithophel may have been correct.

"Perhaps I didn't possess the stamina to stand alone against the testimonies of the many who were my accusers and who held documents that supported their charges. So here I am now, suspended in midair, halfway between the bridge above me and the frigid river that waits for me below."

While struggling with his condemnation, he heard another voice. He looked in the direction of the voice, and again he saw no one. But the voice was strong, and it continued.

"Greetings, Robert, my name is Saul. I was the first king of the Israelites. I was tall and strong with an appearance quite befitting a king of such a great nation as God's people, Israel."

"And still, I did just what you are doing right now, I took my life, and I am sent here to share my story with you. I don't always understand the ways of our wonderful and forgiving God, and especially now, I don't know why He sent me here to speak with you. It would seem to me to be much too late for conversation. But I learned long ago the hard way that His ways are always right, and obedience to His instructions is surely much better than our self-righteous decisions or any sacrifices we make to justify those decisions. I first became aware of that fact from the severe rebuke I received from the great prophet Samuel. He scolded me that obedience to the dictates of God was much better and more pleasing to our God than the sacrifice I offered to Him."

"So listen carefully to my words, Robert. This predicament that you are in is because you have allowed yourself to be overcome with self-pity. You have given in completely to the influence of that pity rather than heed the inner strength of yourself calling out from the deep fortitude of your manhood. Your innate utterances were trying in vain to summon you to live and not die. Instead, you fell prey to the torment and anguish of a ruined reputation; you felt you could not face what was to come. I, on the other hand, yielded to my sanctimonious pride and arrogance when I took my life."

"After all, I was the King, I was a man of power and authority with every right, so I thought, to take matters of all kinds into my own hands. And so I did. Even though it meant taking my own life, I could not permit another, especially an enemy, to do so by their will. If they took my life, it would have to be because I gave the command. You may have read my story, Robert, in your sacred text, but hear it now first hand, from me."

"I was in a war against Israel's most bitter enemies, the Philistines, a strong and ruthless people. There was constant friction and combativeness between the Philistines and the Israelites. This particular time in this specific battle, I, as Israel's King, was directly engaged in combat against the Philistine army. My army was being dreadfully defeated by the Philistine army to the point that many of my men were turning away from battle in retreat mode, running in fear away from the Philistines."

"This was the most shameful act of war; soldiers who abandoned the battlefield in fear like that were not fit to live. Therefore, many soldiers who were strong men filled with integrity and honor, chose to end their own lives whenever it appeared they would be killed in battle rather than tolerate death at the hands or devices of a wicked enemy. So there I was, King of Israel, in a fierce battle which had just robbed me of the lives of my three sons. And I had been so severely wounded that I was at the brink of imminent death. I simply could not permit those ungodly, heathenistic Philistines to defeat me in battle and then mock me further by openly slaying me while surrounded by and in full view of the remaining few of my soldiers."

"My sense of manly honor dictated that I needed to be the one who would make the final determination as to when and how I would die. Therefore, it seemed to me that suicide was the more honorable approach to an eminently unavoidable death. It gave me some small sense of power and control, since I could not forget the

words of the prophet Samuel, who had told me just the night before battle that I and my sons
would die on this very day."

"Prophet Samuel was perturbed with me because I secured the assistance of a witch in the city of Endor to contact him from his place in the grave. In doing so, I disturbed him by having the witch call him out from his grave, and he didn't like it. He asked me why I had disturbed him, and I replied that I needed to be advised concerning the war against the Philistines because the Lord had not responded to my petition when I sought Him for advice. So, instead of waiting for God to respond to me, I consulted a medium for guidance."

Speaking further, Saul said, "The Lord does not like being set aside when guidance is needed, and He abhors having it sought out from anyone other than Himself or His prophets. I grieve all over again, Robert, when I reminisce about how I completely circumvented the counsel of God and deliberately avoided seeking His prophets."

At this point in his narration, Saul became intensely repentant about this ruinous decision and lamented deeply that he had so displeased his God. He was sadly and acutely aware that his prideful stubbornness had been the cause of his premature death. "I did this," Saul said, "because I felt the need to take matters into my own hands about my death. I ordered my armor bearer to take his sword and plunge it through me to hasten my departure from this life. It was my thinking that this action would have given me control over my death and would have preserved my dignity and supported my reputation as a brave military leader."

"Are you able to understand my position, Robert? Can you see what my point of view was at that time concerning the matter? My story is written in your sacred texts. The book named after Prophet Samuel says my armor bearer was too frightened to obey my command to kill me, but instead killed himself with his own sword after witnessing me force myself onto my sword to pierce myself so that I would die. But after piercing myself, I was still not dead. Yet, I was so near to it that I wished desperately for the swift finality of earthly life. It couldn't come fast enough. And while I was in the agonizing throes of near death, a young man came close by and I commanded him to complete my attempted suicide. He obliged me, and did so."

Saul continued his oration, saying, "Even though Samuel had warned me that I would join him in the world of the dead, I didn't take his warning seriously, but I now know that taking my life was still not the will of our Lord. He could very easily have forgiven me and spared me if I had repented with a sincere heart. He's that kind of God, and He and I have conversed about that very subject many times since the day I took the matter of ending my life into my own hands. And just as He was not pleased about my decision to bring my life to an end, He was also not pleased with your decision to do the same. But He is giving you an amazing opportunity to see your wrongdoing. He has sent me to you to share my story."

"I don't know what the outcome is going to be for you, but our merciful God is forgiving and willing to grant us many opportunities to correct our errors and make matters right. You stand, or rather I should say you stood, in a very significant and powerful position. You were a pastor, and as such, had the respect of the members of your congregation just as a king has the respect of the people within the nation over which he rules."

"God holds people like you and me to a higher standard of behavior and a stronger bond of trust and understanding between Him and ourselves. He is the one who places us in our positions and reminds us, many times, that He is always available to help us manage our jobs as leaders. Our God stands always ready to give us the wisdom we need to make our way through the problems that come with the tasks of difficult decision-making and leadership."

"I lost my trust in our God, Robert. I didn't allow myself the time and patience to wait for His directions because I didn't think He was moving fast enough. I thought it was taking much too long for Him to answer my queries, and after all, I had a battle to fight, I had a war on my hands, and I couldn't find Him. He was silent. You were also engaged in a war, different from what I faced, but still a war was raging against you nonetheless, and you didn't wait long enough for God's instructions or help."

"I'm not criticizing you, because I know just how you feel; I did the same as you did. I'm just trying to offer you some comfort and advice, and although it might be too late, I'm offering it anyway. So now I will leave you with that piece of advice. My assignment here with you is finished, but I am grateful for this opportunity to meet you and share my story with you. I don't like the circumstances that brought me here to you, but I've been around long enough to understand that our Beloved God always knows best and always has a plan and reason for His actions. Good-bye Robert."

Here again, Robert was stunned as he hung there shivering in the cold night air while he hovered between his former life on the bridge above him and his future death beneath him in the frigid waters waiting to swallow him up in their watery embrace. What had possibly gone wrong? He had thrown himself off the bridge, and yet he was still alive in some sort of mystical state of being, engaging in one-way conversations with strange men he knew only from scripture who were inexplicably appearing and disappearing.

"What is happening?" Robert asked aloud to no one in particular, "Why am I not dead by now? "

Chapter 4
The Third Encounter

"So now what do I do?" Robert asked himself. "Am I going to fall or not?"

He was becoming more frantic as time passed by, wondering what could possibly come next as he languished in his strange, indeterminate state of existence. Reasoning to himself, he began bemoaning his life. "I was unsuccessful in life as a Pastor, and now I find myself unsuccessful yet again, even in my attempted suicide. Why did life have to be so difficult? And why are my efforts now being thwarted? I don't understand, I can't figure it out, I'm still overwhelmed. Why? I thought that by now everything would be over, the pain of accusations, the stress, and the feelings of not being at my best, I thought I would be free of all those human problems by now, but I'm not. I'm not! Oh God, what is happening to me? I'm trying to end it all, and I can't even do that! I hurled myself off a bridge for God's sake, what more could I possibly have done?"

"You've done quite enough already, young man," came a stern voice. "Oh no," Robert screamed out, "not another one." "Yes, another one," came the retort. "You're trying to do what countless millions have successfully done before you, and for some reason, God is granting you a unique opportunity. He didn't grant me one, but alas, He's giving you this unheard of opportunity. My name is Zimri, and I've been summoned from a distance far back before the time of Christ to visit you. I was a soldier, and being in combat was my specialty. I loved the smell of battle, I thrived on it and was quite successful at it, even if I had to resort to lies, trickery, and deceit. But that was who I was. I was a rogue and a murderer. I plotted against Elah, one of Israel's kings; I waited one night until he got good and drunk, then I murdered him so I could become king of Israel."

"I didn't stop there; after murdering Elah, I went after his father, Baasha, and murdered him. I then slaughtered every single male in Baasha's family. Some of those men were my friends, some were my relatives, but I didn't spare any of them; I killed them all. After becoming king, for a very short while, I might add, while I was ruling in Tirzah, the Israelite army that was camped nearby heard about my murderous rampage against Elah, Baasha, and all the men of Baasha's family. So they made General Omri their King of Israel instead of me, and came after me and invaded my city of Tirzah. Knowing what they would do to me if they caught me, I ran like a scared rabbit. I ran into the fort of the Royal Palace and set it on fire with me in it."

"That's how I died, Robert; I deliberately burned myself to cinders. But I died the way I lived. I deserved to die a violent death because of the willful and merciless violence I committed against others during my lifetime. My legacy will forever include my senseless, heartless killings, and my acts of ruthlessness will always be my burden to bear for all eternity; that is how I will be remembered."

"But for you, Robert, none of those cold-blooded characteristics are attached to your reputation. You were upstanding and respected; in fact, you and I are complete opposites in personality and purpose. Yet you threw it all away, because you couldn't stand the test. I'm not saying it was an easy test because it wasn't; I'm simply saying you should have held on just a little longer to receive your reprieve. In fact, right now, as we speak, the main perpetrators of the conspiracy against you are being exposed, but you're not there to enjoy the benefits of your dropped charges."

"You're about to be vindicated, Robert, but you're not in the place you should be to celebrate your vindication. Your suicidal hastiness is causing much heartache and guilt for those you left behind as they attempt to unravel the complexity of it all. There are all sorts of feelings floating around within the hearts and minds of your family members and the congregation of your church. Some are angry, some are both angry and sad at the same time, some are numb, and some are guilt-ridden for not believing you."

"Your wife, Julia, is devastated and has not eaten or slept since your car was found at the peak of the bridge with the door open, and your hat was found floating in the river. And this is not a good thing for her, because she just found out this morning that the two of you were about to become parents again after trying for so long to have a second child. Just 2 months along, she had prepared a special dinner for you and Bob Jr. to share the good news with the two of you; to tell Bob Jr. that he was going to become a big brother and you were to become a daddy again. But her dinner sat on the stove, untouched and getting cold, Robert because you never came home."

"But possibly the one suffering the most is your beloved son Bob Jr., who's experiencing the most excruciating guilt of his life. His words to you, which caused you such anguish, *Surely Dad, everyone can't be lying, what's up?* are replaying themselves in his head over and over and are causing him torturous guilt and remorse like he's never felt before. And you are not there to comfort him and tell him you understand and that you still love him. Guilt can be a most destructive emotion, especially when it is unresolved, and guilt is what you're leaving your firstborn to wrestle with for the remainder of his life. Your life had purpose and providence, but you have sabotaged all that was destined for you. You have also interrupted the entrance of your third and youngest child into the world, who was to become a woman of great power and influence. She was destined to become a strong contributor to the far-reaching greatness of your ministry and legacy. Was it worth it, Robert?

Even if the accusations had been true, was suicide the answer? What will the people you've counselled think when they learn of your suicide? And what of the people who were served and helped at the Suicide Prevention Agency you established? How will they react when they hear of your disregard for your own words of counsel?

Robert began to sob and wail audibly. "What have I done?" He screamed. "What have I done?" The sound of his haunting and mournful weeping echoed all around him in thunderous reverberations. The voice of his laments mocked him with riotous and boisterous accusations.

"Yes, Robert, look at what you've done!

Consider well and see what you've done!

Who's sorry now, Robert?

You are!

Who have you hurt now, Robert?

Your family!"

Suddenly and involuntarily, Robert began to spin like a top in wild and high-speed circles as if attempting to drown out the noisy rush and power of his own mocking voices. He put his hands up to his ears to lessen the sound of the voices, but he felt his hands being forcefully pulled away from his ears. "You must hear this," a loud voice said, "You have to reckon with both your conscience and your inner voice; they have joined themselves together to become one piercingly loud external voice to confront you face-to-face with what you have just done. You took a life! And you had no right to, even though that life was your own."

Unexpectedly and without warning, the invisible, intangible bottom dropped out, and he felt himself falling. No longer suspended in mid-air as just a short while ago, but now he was falling as he did when he first left the bridge, but this time at a more alarming rate of speed and feet first this time. "Oh God, please help me," Robert heard himself trying to say as he pierced the surface of the freezing water like a directional torpedo. His words were garbled as his fall plunged him into the water, which sucked him in like a vortex and forced him straight downward into the dark and unbelievably cold depths of the river.

Still fully alert and completely aware of what was happening, Robert wondered why he had not lost all consciousness at this point. Instead, he was totally immersed in the cold river with an array of sea creatures swimming about him as if unaware of his presence, as if he were or was invisible. He was bewildered beyond all reason as he recounted his steps from the moment he left the bridge until now. By all human logic and every rule of the universe, he should be dead, yet he was still very much alive.

Then, appearing out of nowhere and swimming directly toward him, Robert saw the most gargantuan thing he had ever seen. It was not swimming in an aimless and wandering sort of manner as the other sea creatures were, but it was headed directly toward Robert as though he were the round center of a bull's eye target. And with calm but intentional motion, this thing opened its hugely enormous mouth as it continued to swim with a purpose straight at Robert.

He tried desperately to run away from this sea monster, but could not. Then, realizing that running underwater was next to impossible, and more frightened than he had ever been, Robert tried madly to swim away. But he was no match for this massive underwater beast. Even with its slow and deliberate determination, the creature's pace was faster and stronger than his as it fixed its purposeful aim and attention on Robert. In an instant, he felt himself being engulfed in complete and utter darkness. He had been swallowed.

"Where am I," Robert ~~he~~ called out in fear, "Am I in hell?" "No, you're not in hell," the answer came back. "You're inside of me, I just swallowed you." Hearing this, Robert froze on the spot in horror and dread; his heart began to beat with such a violent and vigorous force that it seemed it was going to come completely out of his body or stop beating altogether from sheer fright. In a state of absolute terror, Robert screamed and cried and shrieked at the top of his lungs, "HELP ME! SOMEBODY PLEASE! HELP ME!" He was hysterical.

Realizing Robert's crazed state of mind, the sea creature tried to lessen his fear by encouraging him to calm down. This admonition only heightened his overwrought state all the more. "HELP ME, HELP ME, HELP ME," he shouted over and over; "GET ME OUT OF HERE, PLEASE, SOMEBODY PLEASE, HELP ME, GET ME OUT OF HERE."

He was losing his voice, getting lightheaded, and entering into a state of near collapse. Then, plainly and without pity, the three voices of Ahithophel, Saul, and Zimri spoke to Robert in unison, "I thought you wanted to kill yourself." This unsympathetic and indifferent reminder seemed to assuage Robert's panic and remind him of the real reason he was in this awful place. He alone was responsible for his predicament; he alone had brought himself to this wretched place. He could blame no one else but himself. The reckoning of his direct responsibility for his current situation began to slowly bring him back down from his self-induced emotional frenzy.

Seizing the moment to take advantage of Robert's diminishing hysteria, the sea creature begins to speak. "Robert, I need to explain what is going on now and why you are here inside of me. I am that same great fish that God prepared to swallow Jonah. You remember Jonah's story; you've preached it several times. God designed me with a uniqueness that allows me to swallow a man and permit him to remain alive inside of me for as long as God says he should. I am designed to bring in fresh oxygen for whoever I swallow, so they can breathe and stay alive while in me. And on God's command, I will regurgitate him up at whatever location God designates."

"After my time with Jonah, God sent me to live in the beautiful, cool, refreshing waters of Eden to enjoy life while waiting for my next assignment. And that's where I've been living for the past several millennia, waiting for this day when you would throw yourself from a bridge into the icy river. So when you did, God called me and I swam quickly from Eden to these waters beneath the bridge from which you jumped, and I waited there in the river for you. Once your three visits were completed and you ceased to hover in mid-air, I swam to the spot where you would fall so we could meet, or rather, so I could swallow you. It was not my intention, however, to frighten you, sorry about that, Robert; I was just answering the call of God and following His orders."

Stunned and bewildered, Robert began questioning his circumstances and surroundings once again. "Is this creature actually talking to me, or am I hearing things out of simple delirium resulting from my fall into the river? I'm trying to kill myself, and instead of dying, I'm being confronted by biblical personages telling me about their suicidal episodes, and now this. Here I am somewhere at the bottom of the river, supposedly in the belly of a huge sea monster who claims to be the same big fish that swallowed Jonah. How absurd is that? This can't be real, but it certainly feels like it is."

"It is quite real, Robert, I assure you it is," answered the fish. Startled at the sea creature's quick response, yet still unable to come to grips with what was happening to him, Robert lamented again.

"Oh my God, I can't believe this is real, maybe I am dead after all; and if I am dead, I know without a doubt that death is very real. I just never thought it would be like this. I don't know what I imagined it would be, but surely not this. Oh God, what do I do now? I'm standing here in complete darkness, not knowing what will happen next, or what I should do next, or whether I am destined to be in this predicament for the rest of eternity."

At this point, the fish spoke again. "Well, Robert, you're on the right track, you're seeking God for answers, and that's how it should be. Our God intended your life to be lived with gusto and with confidence in Him who makes all things possible. He wanted there to be a deep and abiding love between all of humanity and Himself. Also included in His plan was for each of you to love yourselves and appreciate yourselves as the amazingly intricate beings that you are. After all, He fashioned you very carefully and delicately and created a world for you to live in with abundant resources for your continued existence. In fact, when He created and formed this earth, it was not for the purpose of existing as an empty place, but He intended that it should be inhabited, lived in, and enjoyed."

"But, I will be silent now so you can have your time with our LORD. However, before I cease to speak, I need to remind you, as a point of clarity, that I am a fish, not a sea creature nor sea monster, but a fish specially prepared and fashioned by God. So get that straight, before you proceed in conversation with Him. He doesn't like to have His creations disregarded or disrespected with sarcasm and intentional mislabeling. I am a fish, Robert, remember that, and in particular, remember where you are." Robert felt a distinct cold chill run up and down his spine at the admonishment of the fish to 'remember where you are.' Those words left him with no other choice but to reckon with and remember exactly where he was, how he had gotten there, and to accept his responsibility for being in this predicament. He was entirely at fault and could blame no one else but himself. Remembering the story of Jonah, he repented for having judged the prophet so harshly in his sermons and for labelling him a disobedient and willful servant of God who pretty much deserved what he received in the form of his underwater ordeal. But now that he found himself in the same place as Jonah had been millennia ago, he began to do the same thing Jonah did—he began to pray.

"Oh God, I'm sorry. I'm sorry I was so hasty with my decision to end my life when things got rough. You gave me life, Lord, and I disregarded it as if it meant nothing to me. I threw it away as if it were trash to be disposed of. So now, God, I am begging for Your forgiveness. I'm calling on You for help. And although I'm not even sure what kind of help I'm asking for, I'm just asking and pleading for help because You know what kind of help I need and what kind will make a difference here. So I'm just asking, please help me. I acknowledge my wrongdoing in committing this awful sin against You, against myself as Your man of God, and against Your purpose and plans for my life. I acted as though I had the authority to do what I did, but I now realize that I didn't. And for this, I am so very sorry. Oh God, please forgive me. I know I'm rambling, God, but I don't know what else to do or how to say what I need to say or even what I should say, for that matter."

Sobbing almost uncontrollably, Robert continued. "God, You have never failed me, even in life; You were always there. Even when I thought sometimes that You had gone far from me, I soon realized that You had not left me at all. You just wanted me to grow up and be the man You were making me. I know I failed this test miserably, so I'm asking for another chance Oh God. I promise if You give me another chance, I'll stand up and be a man and face my accusers like the man You want me to be. I'm sorry, God, for putting my family through this by having Julia go through this all alone without me. God, I'm sorry that I will never see the beautiful child you are blessing us with, and for leaving this innocent, unborn infant such a cowardly legacy. I won't even be there to explain my case or my actions. I'm sorry for leaving this unpleasant task in Julia and Bob's hands; it is so unfair to them."

"But Lord, You have been such a wonderful God, so what happens now to our relationship? Will You hold this against me, or will You forgive me?"

With his face drenched in tears, Robert ceased to pray as he waited to hear what God had to say in response to his prayers and pleadings. Will God answer him? Has God even heard his lament? He waited... it is silent. The wait seemed like an eternity, but he had no choice but to wait; he had nowhere to go and no schedules to keep, so he waited.

Chapter 5
Conversations with God

Robert was still waiting to hear from God, and it seemed as though several hours had passed since he ended his prayerful pleadings. Here again, he began to mutter to himself.

"I feel as though I'm just waking up from a very long night's sleep. But there is no way to determine the accuracy of what I'm feeling because I'm still inside Jonah's fish, and there is only darkness in here. There's no visible connection to even the dim light of the underwater world, nor any way for me to know whether it's daylight or nighttime above the river. And I'm still not dead yet! With everything that I've experienced since the bridge, I'm still alive despite my attempt to end my life. So I have no choice but to wait here until a change of some sort happens. Maybe I'm destined to suffocate right here inside this fish. Maybe that's how I'll die. But there's probably a very remote chance of that happening since I've already been in here for quite a while and my breathing is not the least bit adversely affected at all."

No sooner had he completed his sentence when suddenly and without warning, from deep within the bowels of the earth, from the heavens above, and all directions around him came the most commanding and earth-shattering sound Robert had ever heard. He knew immediately it was the voice of God. He had heard God speak to him before through the Word of Scripture, through songs, his inner voice, prophetic words, and other supernatural means. But this! This thunderous, quaking, earth shaking sound accompanied by such vehement reverberation, was a unique sound that he had never heard before; yet he knew instinctively it was indeed the voice of God.

Every being, life form, dead thing, inanimate thing, and type of matter knows the voice of God. Robert fell flat on his face in a prostrate position at the realization that he was hearing God in the belly of this great fish, where it was no longer midnight dark but was illuminated with the brightest light he had ever seen. No electrical lighting, nor solar-powered device could compare to the brilliance of this illumination. Not even

Hollywood could replicate this. And Robert lay on his face, not daring to look up because he knew he was in the presence of God.

Then he heard God call his name. "*Robert*? *What are you doing here in this place*?" Trembling as he never had before, Robert was too afraid to answer, yet too afraid not to. Still flat on his face, he opened his mouth in an attempt to answer God, but nothing would come out. Try as he may, he could not utter a sound. Again, God demanded, "*Robert, why are you here in this place*?" He was now drenched in a cold sweat, attempting to answer God; so he opened his mouth and tried again to speak, but all that he could say was, "I... I"... and nothing more. He thought God would force him to speak, but instead there was only silence, no words from the Lord.

There was only complete silence! Robert felt unnerved by God's silence and knew that it would be in his best interest to answer God. He reminded himself that not responding to God was definitely not the thing to do. So as he inhaled deeply in preparation to reply, his words came gushing forth from his mouth like water being released from a dam.

Without taking a breath, he blurted, "Oh God I was so overwhelmed with what was happening in my life because I was being accused of something I didn't do and nobody believed me not even my son Bob and my wife doubted me too and my congregation was falling apart because of it and the news media and social media and TV were all carrying stories that made me look guilty and ruining my reputation and I couldn't prove my innocence and I just couldn't take any more, so I decided to end it all by committing suicide. And that's why I just let myself fall from the bridge!"

Completely breathless, Robert took in a long, gasping breath. More silence!

"Did God hear me?" Robert mumbled to himself.

"I heard you, Robert, and now I have a few questions for you." God replied.

"Oh God," Robert groaned.

"Yes, I AM He," God responded, *"and I will ask you these questions:*

"Why did you choose to take the wicked and cowardly advice of that lying accuser?

How did you not recognize his deceitful and reprehensible voice?

Why did you not use the free will I gave you to choose life over death?

Did I ever grant you permission to take a life, even when that life was your own?

Answer me, Robert; you've made your choice, now answer me!"

Robert was speechless. He didn't know how to answer God, especially now that he was finally hearing Him so clearly. "But where was God when I so desperately needed Him?" he pondered.

"I was right there with you, Robert, just as I was all of the many other times. I made a promise to you never to leave you or abandon you, and I AM a keeper of my word. My words go out of my mouth and do not return unaccomplished, annulled, or cancelled. The words that I've spoken are established permanently and forever,

With what was left of his strength, Robert tried to answer God's questions, but to no avail. He was much too weak to even look up, or to open his mouth, or utter a response. There was only the quiet presence of the absence of sound, total silence!

Not knowing what to do, but remembering instinctively that prayer had always been a source of encouraged enlightenment for him, Robert assumed the position of kneeling prayer and began to pray with an earnestness that he had never felt before.

"O God, in my distress and calamities I have
called on You in times past...
I called on You whenever I needed help...

When everything seemed impossible and
insurmountable...
I called on Your name...

When I felt as if I was drowning in a sea of trouble...

As if I was losing my breath...

As if I could not survive any longer...

As if everything around me was sinking and pulling me down with it...

When I felt like I was in a deep pit with no way out...

When I couldn't even see the light of the sky above me...

When I kept looking and saw nothing, kept hoping and felt nothing...

When it seemed like my life was slipping away...

As if I was isolated and completely alone...

It was during those times, Lord, that You came to me...

Lord, You made Your presence known to me...

You comforted me then and gave me peace...

Now, Lord, I need You more than those times...

I need Your forgiveness...

I need Your help in this impossible situation that I've put myself in...

And even if You choose not to get me out of it...just please forgive me...

I acknowledge my sin; I had no right to take my life...

Because my life was not my own…
You gave it to me with a purpose to fulfill…
So forgive me, Lord, I pray."

Then, out of the abyss of silence came the commanding yet comforting voice of the Lord.

"Yes, of course, I forgive you, Robert. I love you too much not to. And your repentant heart I cannot ignore, I respond to repentance and contrite spirits. You are mine, Robert, and I AM yours, and my love for you is constant and everlasting and much stronger and greater than your sin. Take comfort and know that I have forgiven you, know that I still love you, and know that I have never stopped loving you, nor will I ever stop loving you. I AM compassionate, I AM merciful, and I AM the forgiver of sins. I AM the only true and living God, I AM eternal and everlasting, and I AM without end or beginning. I exist forever, Robert, by My power and might, there is none like Me, and your sin of self-murder is forgiven."

Robert was instantly relieved; he felt cleansed. He knew he had just been gently scrubbed and washed of the soil and condemnation of every wrong action, every unkind thought, every wayward word, and every ungodly behavior he had ever committed. He exhaled a deep sigh of relief and experienced a sense of profound gratefulness to God for having been forgiven. "But I wonder," he thought, "if God will restore my life back to its former place before I contemplated suicide." Summoning up every bit of his courage, he appealed to God. "Oh Lord, I know what I'm about to ask is impossible by human standards, but I also know that nothing is impossible with You. Inhaling deeply, he continued, so Oh Lord God, since nothing is impossible with You, I'm asking if You can restore my life back to the place it was before my suicidal act? "

"You are so very right, Robert, nothing is impossible with Me, and yes, I can restore you to your former place in life."

Robert then dared to ask the Lord one more clarifying question. "Lord, God of heaven, earth and all things, I know that You CAN restore my life back, but, WILL You restore my life back?" Robert cringed at the very audacity of his question and again began to ponder over the terrible fall-out from what he had done. He realized the unfair burden he had placed on the shoulders and in the hearts of the many people who looked up to him and trusted him to be a sound and stable example of practical thinking and sensible judgments. He had failed miserably to measure up to those standards. But still, he waited for an answer from God. Then finally! He heard God!

"You ask me if I will restore your life to its former place. You are a man into whom I placed an abundance of intellect and understanding. I have granted you many opportunities to study my laws of physics and my laws of reciprocity, and my processing of seasons. You have learned well how this earth and its elements respond to the actions and exploits of my sons and daughters, for whom I created this beautiful earth as their habitation."

"You understand well that every action, every thought, every conversation, and every behavior carries its own set of consequences. Some consequences are reversible, others are not. Some consequences are pleasant, others are not. Some consequences bring great joy, others bring great sadness. Some consequences are temporary, others are permanent. And because I AM God and God alone, I have set the criterion by which all consequential laws of this earth, the galaxies, their substances, their contents, and all life forms and matter are bound. And while I have permitted my sons and daughters to discover a few of the hidden

workings, meanings, and essences of a few of these things, I have long ago determined that all of these things are subject to my laws of reciprocity and consequence."

"So, Robert, because you asked me if I would restore your life to its former place, I will answer your question with a question of my own. Since you threw away the life I gave you and abdicated your place among the living, choosing rather to be with the dead, what do you think your consequences should be?"

Bone-chilling sensations began emerging from within Robert's being. He dared not ask God another question. Then gradually, the brightness of God's presence began to diminish, only to be replaced by the cool darkness of the fish's belly. Then, he clearly heard God say, *"I still love you, Robert, I always will!"* And for that brief moment when God spoke, His brightness was again visible for just that flash in time.

Chapter 6
The Conclusion of the Matter

Cloaked in the darkness of the fish's belly, Robert lay face down, repentant and confused. He had no idea what was to come next, after all God had spoken, so there was nothing left to do or say but Amen to the words of the Lord.

Lying there in complete remorse, Robert once again began to entertain myriad thoughts in his head. He realized that his decision to end his life was not the thing he should have done. In contemplation, he mused, "I should have stood firm in my innocence, I should have withstood the criticisms, I should have allowed time to uncover the truth and prove all things. But I was hasty, I was at a low and vulnerable point in my life; my strength had been sapped, and I had become severely weakened by all the negativity surrounding me. I relied too heavily on my six-sigma training instead of on God, who is more than able in every situation. I regretfully didn't give much thought to how my decision would affect my wife, my son, and everyone else who loved me; indeed, my act was selfish in every respect. So now, according to God, I must bear the consequences of my actions."

With a gentle tenor in his voice, the fish spoke again. "Well, my assignment is almost complete. I need to deliver you now to the place where God has instructed me to take you. I don't know if it is to the realm of the dead or back to the world of the living, I just know I was told to take you to a particular location. And when I deliver you to your destination, I am going back to the beautiful waters of Eden to live there while I wait for my next assignment. Are you ready? Prepare to go now because I'm ready to deliver you. And goodbye, Robert, it has been my honor to have participated in your encounter with God. I probably will not ever see you again, so go in peace."

Robert did not answer. What would be the point? At this juncture in time, he felt helpless to make any determination about anything pertaining to his whereabouts, his past, his present, or his future. He was at the mercy of the consequences, whatever they might be, that he alone had set in motion; so he just remained silent and waited. And as he waited, he remembered a song his mother used to sing, "Que-sera-sera-whatever-will-be-will-be-the-future's-not-ours-to-see-que-sera-sera..." Indeed, he knew with a certainty that his future was quite uncertain.

Then unexpectedly, great surges of movement and wrenching sounds began to take place. Robert felt himself being forcefully pushed along as though many giant, turbulent ocean waves were thrusting him forward. No longer in control of his movements, he felt himself being thrashed about inside the fish's belly, and he wondered if he was about to be vomited up onto some designated place as Jonah had been vomited up onto the shore according to the instructions of God.

With everything that had happened to him since he left the bridge, Robert was quite aware that he had relinquished all rights to have any say about what would occur next. So he relaxed as best he could under the circumstances and allowed himself to be swept along by these forceful currents to a place unknown. From a distance, he could see patches of what appeared to be daylight. And very quickly, these patches merged together to appear as one huge single opening. He felt as if he was inside a dark cave looking outward toward the cave's open entrance, and he was being very swiftly propelled by the rush of moving waters to that opening.

Finally, from out of the fish's belly, through the fish's mouth, he was forcefully ejected so that he landed flat on his back with his face turned upward. And although his eyes were still closed, Robert perceived it to be daylight wherever he was. Then, from a distance, he heard a faint but familiar voice of a woman calling his name.

"Robert... Robert, honey!" He knew this voice; it was his mother's voice, but his mother had died three years ago. He was grateful that she had not lived to witness the ordeal of suspicion and allegations he'd gone through. But why was he now hearing her calling his name? Then he heard it again, "Robert...Robert, honey!" But this time the voice was that of his wife Julia, and she was very much alive. Again, he heard his name, "Robert... Robert, honey!" As he lay there on the soft ground listening to the voice calling out to him, he reasoned, "If it's Mom, I'm dead; if it's Julia, I've been granted another chance." Slowly and with trepidation, Robert managed to open his eyes. And as his eyes adjusted to the light, he looked up and saw the beautiful face of the woman calling his name.

About the Author

Rev. Dr. Sheila Robinson is the granddaughter of a Pentecostal Pastor. She holds RN in nursing from Flushing, Medical Center, a Master of Arts degree in Pastoral Ministries from Fuller Theological Seminary and a Doctor of Ministry degree from San Francisco Theological Seminary.

Her broadcasting career ~~that~~ spanned ~~nearly~~ 30 years in which she hosted a Sunday morning Gospel Music radio show in the San Francisco Bay Area. She ~~and~~ co-founded and served as the first President of the Bay Area Religious Announcers Guild. Additionally, she is a nine-time recipient of the Best Religious Announcer Award from the Bay Area Gospel Academy Awards Ceremony and was inducted into the Academy Hall of Fame.

Dr. Robinson was invited to attend the US/China Joint Conference on Women's Issues in Beijing, China. She blended her nursing expertise and commitment to ministry in a medical and evangelistic outreaches in Jamaica, West Indies, and to the Kingdom of Jordan, where she saw first-hand the Biblical sites referenced in Scripture, and experienced a profound spiritual moment by being rebaptized in the historic waters of the Jordan River.

She has authored several volumes including a *children's* poetry, song, and activity book with an accompanying audio tape entitled, *From Auntie Sheila*, and a book of poems entitled, *My Perfect God*. Her novels include *Those Old Women: Tell Their Stories*, *Jennifer's Distant Journey*, and two forthcoming volumes: *They Speak for Themselves: Biblical Women Tell Their Own Stories and The Reunion: Reliving the Experiences of Biblical Women*. She is also a contributing writer of Life Lessons/Insight Essays for the *Women of Color Study Bible* for which received the Peninsula Book Club Award for excellence among African American writers. Dr. Robinson was a feature writer for the (San Jose) *City Flight News Magazine*, and the *Oakland Post*.

As a registered nurse, Dr. Robinson understands from first-hand clinical experience the complex emotional trauma associated with suicide and unsuccessful suicide attempts.

Contact Information

~~dr~~.sheilafrobinson@gmail.com

www.ingramcontent.com/pod-product-compliance
Lightning Source LLC
Chambersburg PA
CBHW071841190726
48292CB00005B/1864